What's My Superpower?

For the superhero mother-daughter duo, Stacey and Nalajoss.

Published by Inhabit Media Inc. · www.inhabitmedia.com

Inhabit Media Inc. (Iqaluit), P.O. Box 11125, Iqaluit, Nunavut, X0A 1H0 · (Toronto), 191 Eglinton Avenue East, Suite 301, Toronto, Ontario, M4P 1K1

Design and layout copyright © 2017 Inhabit Media Inc.

Text copyright © 2017 by Aviaq Johnston

Illustrations by Tim Mack copyright © 2017 Inhabit Media Inc.

Editors: Neil Christopher and Kelly Ward

Art director: Danny Christopher

We acknowledge the support of the Canada Council for the Arts for our publishing program.

This project was made possible in part by the Government of Canada.

Library and Archives Canada Cataloguing in Publication

Johnston, Aviaq, author
    What's my superpower? / by Aviaq Johnston ; illustrated
by Tim Mack.

ISBN 978-1-77227-140-9 (hardcover)

    I. Mack, Tim, 1984-, illustrator II. Title. III. Title: What
is my superpower?

PS8619.O4848W53 2017   jC813'.6   C2017-902929-0

Printed in Canada

WHAT'S MY SUPERPOWER?

by Aviaq Johnston • illustrated by Tim Mack

INHABIT
MEDIA

In a little house in the very middle of a small town where winter is always longer than summer, a little girl named Nalvana lived with her mother.

Nalvana loved everything about her small town. She loved the quiet roads with lots of space to play hide-and-seek, and tag, and street hockey. She loved to ride her bike without worrying about cars coming down the road like big monsters.

"*Anaana*," Nalvana said to her mother one day, "if I had a superpower, I could fight big monsters, you know?"

"Yes, *Panik*," her mother replied, as she stroked Nalvana's hair.

"Do you think I'll ever have a superpower?" Nalvana asked.

"I don't know, Panik. Maybe," her mother said with a smile.

Nalvana always thought about what it would be like to have superpowers. Everywhere she went, she wore a yellow cape made from a blanket and a pair of snowmobiling goggles resting on her head.

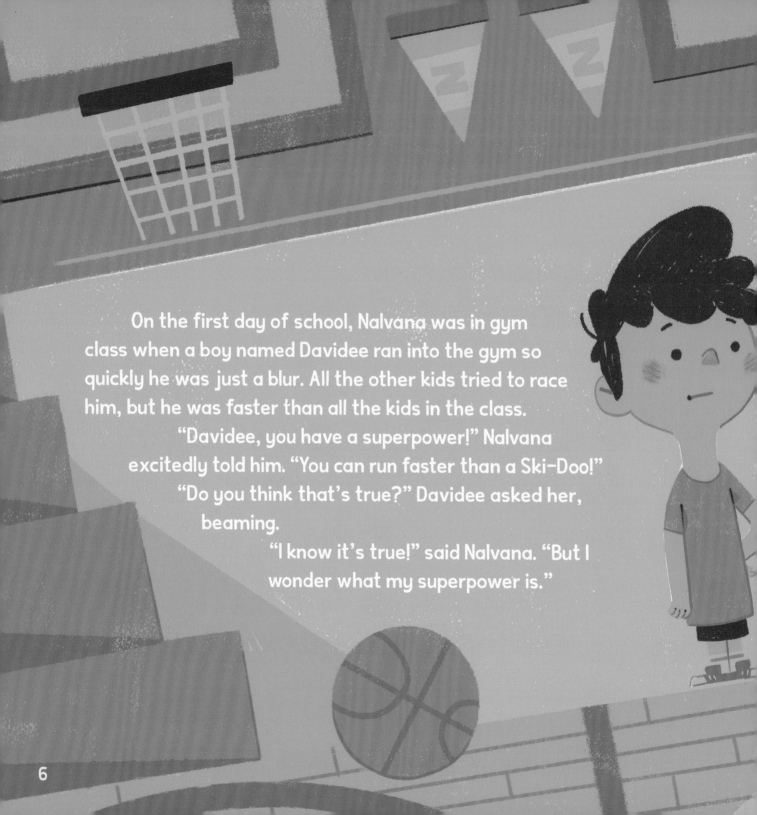

On the first day of school, Nalvana was in gym class when a boy named Davidee ran into the gym so quickly he was just a blur. All the other kids tried to race him, but he was faster than all the kids in the class.

"Davidee, you have a superpower!" Nalvana excitedly told him. "You can run faster than a Ski-Doo!"

"Do you think that's true?" Davidee asked her, beaming.

"I know it's true!" said Nalvana. "But I wonder what my superpower is."

Nalvana went home after school and told her mom all about Davidee.

"He was so fast he almost burned the floor of the gym!" Nalvana told her. "He was like the wind on a blizzardy day."

"Wow, he really must have super speed," her mother replied.

"If Davidee has a superpower, does that mean I can have a superpower, too?" Nalvana asked.

"I'm sure we will find out soon," her mom said.

Nalvana imagined herself flying in the sky, or talking to animals, or even breathing underwater.

The days began to grow colder, but that did not stop Nalvana from going to the playground to play with her friends.

One day, Nalvana saw her friend Maata swinging so high that it looked like she was going to loop around the swing set. Nalvana and her friends all stared at Maata, amazed.

Then suddenly, Maata was flying from the swing! She landed so far away that Nalvana was sure that Maata had flown through the air.

"You can fly! You can fly!" Nalvana said.

Maata smiled widely. "Really?" she asked.

"Of course!" Nalvana said. "If you keep practising, someday you'll be able to fly all the way around the world!"

11

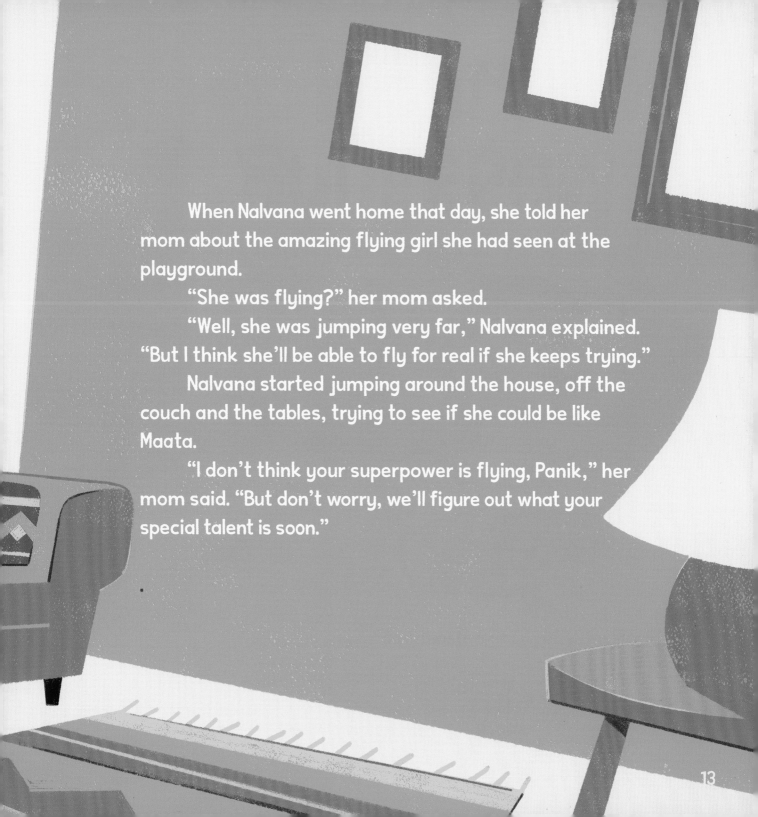

When Nalvana went home that day, she told her mom about the amazing flying girl she had seen at the playground.

"She was flying?" her mom asked.

"Well, she was jumping very far," Nalvana explained. "But I think she'll be able to fly for real if she keeps trying."

Nalvana started jumping around the house, off the couch and the tables, trying to see if she could be like Maata.

"I don't think your superpower is flying, Panik," her mom said. "But don't worry, we'll figure out what your special talent is soon."

The next day, Nalvana and her friends brought their sleds to the big hill next to their school to go sliding.

Nalvana's cousin, Joanasie, was already at the top of the hill building an *inuksuk*. All across the top of the hill, there were snow sculptures of animals and snowmen, and even a whole *iglu*!

"Joanasie, did you make these?" Nalvana asked.

"Yup," he said. "All of them. Even that polar bear right there. It was easy!"

"What else can you make?" she asked.

"Anything! I can make a caribou, and maybe even a monkey. I can make things out of rocks and even ice!"

"Is it your superpower to make things?" Nalvana asked. "Can you build whatever you can think of?"

"Yup," he replied. "I can build anything!"

Nalvana told her mom all about Joanasie's superpower.

"Panik, didn't you know that Joanasie's dad has that superpower, too? Joanasie is going to be a carver just like his father."

"Does that mean I might have that superpower, too?" Nalvana asked. "I've never tried to build anything before!"

"Why don't you try it out?" her mom said.

Nalvana tried to build an inuksuk out of her blocks, but it fell over. She tried to make a house out of her Legos, but it was too hard. She sighed. "I guess it's not my superpower."

Her mom hugged her tight. "I'm sure we'll figure it out soon, Panik."

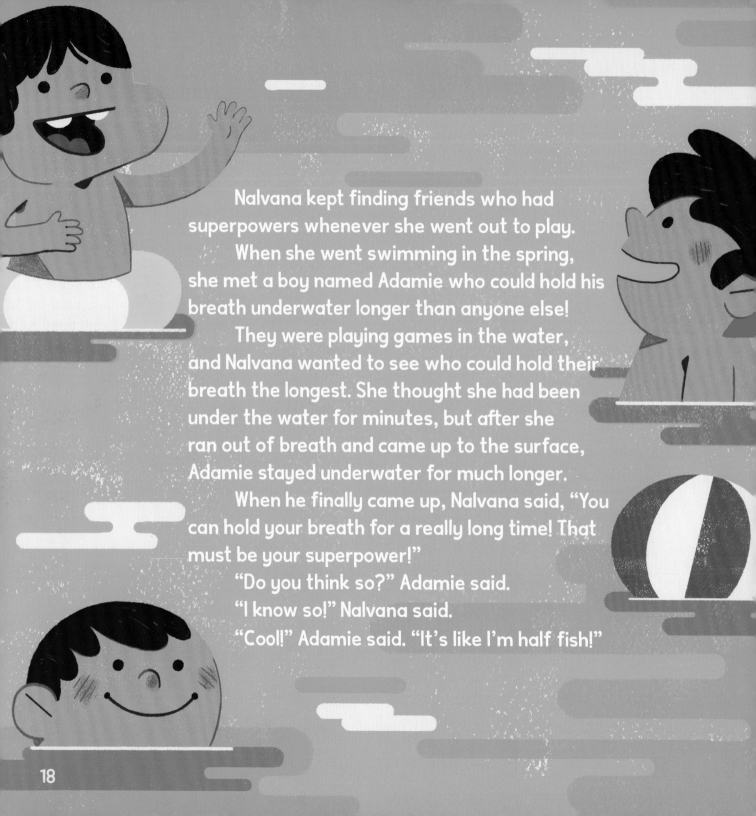

Nalvana kept finding friends who had superpowers whenever she went out to play.

When she went swimming in the spring, she met a boy named Adamie who could hold his breath underwater longer than anyone else!

They were playing games in the water, and Nalvana wanted to see who could hold their breath the longest. She thought she had been under the water for minutes, but after she ran out of breath and came up to the surface, Adamie stayed underwater for much longer.

When he finally came up, Nalvana said, "You can hold your breath for a really long time! That must be your superpower!"

"Do you think so?" Adamie said.

"I know so!" Nalvana said.

"Cool!" Adamie said. "It's like I'm half fish!"

Nalvana was happy for her friends. They had all found the things that they were good at. She liked to tell them they had superpowers, and she liked to see them smile. They all seemed so happy to have a special talent.

But Nalvana wished she knew what her superpower was.

"Anaana," Nalvana said when she came home from school one day. "I still don't know what my superpower is. Am I ever going to figure it out?"

Her mom gave her a big smile.

"I think I know what your superpower is, Panik," she said.

Nalvana looked up at her mom, excited but confused. "What is it? Can I fly like Maata? Or am I really strong?"

"No, Panik, can't you see?" her mother asked as she hugged Nalvana close. "Your superpower is making people feel good about themselves."

Nalvana smiled. "I think that's a good superpower to have," she said.

Inuktitut Glossary:

anaana (a-naa-na): Mother

iglu (ee-glue): A snow house

inuksuk (ee-nook-shook): A sculpture made with rocks piled on top of each other

panik (puh-nick): Daughter

Aviaq Johnston is a young Inuk author from Igloolik, Nunavut. Her debut novel, *Those Who Run in the Sky,* was released in the spring of 2017. In 2014, she won first place in the Aboriginal Arts and Stories competition for her short story "Tarnikuluk," which also earned her a Governor General's History Award. Aviaq is a graduate of Nunavut Sivuniksavut, and she has a diploma in Social Service Work from Canadore College. Aviaq loves to travel and has lived in Australia and Vietnam. She spends most of her time reading, writing, studying, and procrastinating. She goes back and forth between Iqaluit, Nunavut, and Ottawa, Ontario.

Tim Mack cannot fly, run super fast, or swim like a fish, so instead he draws those things. Tim is a Canadian-born illustrator living in Vancouver, British Columbia. He enjoys playing with colours and shapes and never misses an opportunity to swim in the ocean, though he still wishes he could swim as well as a fish.